ABSINTHE

ABSINTHE

A Novel

CHRISTOPHE BATAILLE

TRANSLATED FROM THE FRENCH BY RICHARD HOWARD

TMP

The Marlboro Press/Northwestern
Northwestern University Press
Evanston, Illinois

The Marlboro Press/Northwestern
Northwestern University Press
Evanston, Illinois 60208-4210

Publication of this work was supported in part by the French Ministry of
Culture.

Printed in the United States of America

ISBN 0-8101-6042-0

Library of Congress Cataloging-in-Publication Data

Bataille, Christophe.
   [Absinthe. English]
   Absinthe : a novel / Christophe Bataille ; translated from the
French by Richard Howard.
      p. cm.
   ISBN 0-8101-6042-0 (cloth : alk. paper)
   I. Title.
PQ2662.A842A6313 1999
843'.914—dc21   98-51925
                                                           CIP

The paper used in this publication meets the minimum requirements of
the American National Standard for Information Sciences—Permanence
of Paper for Printed Library Materials, ANSI Z39.48-1984.

Life is cruelly combined with absinthe.

— Mme de Sévigné
Letter of February 17, 1672

OVERTURE

1

It had been a painful winter. The air was dry, and the wind danced across the plain. Snow was everywhere; in places, above a man's head. And glowed, sometimes, in the pale sunshine.

Darkness had fallen between the banks of the Cluse. The men lived like sleepwalkers, and daylight itself seemed stone. Sometimes a candle would appear, its flame rousing fantastic shapes out of the snow. The little troop collected around the cannons. In silence. Only a faint rustle could be heard, near the horizon. The flame was cold, white; it floated in midair. No one breathed. The walls of ice creaked under their own weight. Each man waited for the moment when darkness would sink into the labyrinth and extinguish the candle. It was a gamble.

But that night of February 2, 1871, we heard a cry—in French. Everyone got up, fast; the cannon was already loaded. For several minutes everyone waited. For nothing. A clank of metal grazed the cliffs. A sort of pale ink flowed down, and the candle went out. The men returned to their makeshift shelter: more waiting.

The east wing of the French army was isolated, cut off from Lyon. The night before, it had begun falling back toward Switzerland.

The roads were covered by what looked like long strips of white cotton. The Jura's freezing air drifted among the red and blue uniforms. Retreat was delayed by the winter. The French had to be protected at the bend of the Cluse.

A narrow plain opened between two ramparts of darkness. The Fort of Joux towered above the eastern side: a medieval barracks, heavily barred. Snow blurred its stone ridges.

The fort soon vanished into the storm.

General Bressoles had posted twenty men up there, and a battery of twelve guns. Two eight-bore cannons were brought up to protect the bend of the Cluse. Ninety artillerymen and a company of engineers climbed to Joux. It was dark by then. Water was sprinkled on the snow around the fort; a thick sheet of ice formed, which soon concealed the battery.

A strange thing: the storm dropped, and the air was no longer filled with snow. The rustle of flakes gave way to silence. The temperature fell to fifteen degrees below freezing. Around the cannons, a white horizon devoured everything.

To avoid notice, the French artillerymen lived in silence. Their gestures were sluggish, their vision troubled by this featureless landscape. No one slept; cold had whitened the uniforms. It seemed a company of ghosts. The Fort of Joux was cut off from the world; there were no more hours. The men kept watch by night, then by day: they forgot.

The Germans came up to the bend of the Cluse. A group of French soldiers bravely went down to the plain, and the batteries fired from the fort. The two eight-bore cannons protecting Les Fourgs repulsed the enemy.

The battle lasted several days. The Germans set up four long-range guns they never had a chance to use. They were forced to retreat. Their dead numbered nearly four hundred.

Around Joux, the snow had gradually melted. Ochre patches appeared here and there. But the fighting continued, and the fort's reserves were diminishing; one soldier died. Solitude and cold weighed heavily on the artillerymen. A gun liaison from the 24th

Corps, Jean Mardet, discovered several huge bundles in the cellars where no one had ventured until then.

The rough canvas bags were as light as the wind. They were stuffed with dried petals. Someone recognized the gentians that grew in the valleys west of Pontarlier. They were used to make absinthe.

The French soldiers sucked the petals of the poison flowers. The fighting continued.

The east wing of the army was secure; the Germans evacuated Pontarlier. The sun restored their bright color to the Joux hillsides. When General Bressoles climbed to the fort to greet its courageous defenders, he found only a few ragged survivors.

A strange joy could be read in the dead men's eyes.

2

In the morning, Jean Mardet left the fort and followed the Joux road alone. He was heading toward the Cluse. The sun was white in the distance. After he had walked an hour, Pontarlier came into sight. From the east, the town was gray. The soldier passed men in uniform walking toward him. He did not stop.

He left the French army without a word.

He went into a café that served absinthe. He thought of Lise. Then he turned back and headed toward the Lot, the country of his birth.

Jean Mardet walked for days on end before catching sight of Saint-Cirq-Lapopie. He recognized his house, on the edge of the cliff. The shutters were closed. For a moment, he inhaled the wind—it was almost cool. A pale mist had fallen over the village.

He laid his bundle beside the river, which emitted the melancholy of forgotten waterways. The warmth of the pebbles reminded him of the Fort of Joux. The night was upon him. Naked, Jean slipped into the black water. He moved ahead a few yards, lost his footing, let the current carry him. He couldn't swim.

He washed against some reeds and clung to them, feeling against his body the soft tips of the plants. It was a game from his childhood. He felt pricked all over; he released himself in order to regain the current. The silk flowed through his hands. He closed his eyes, plunging his face into the stream. When he lifted his head from the water, he took a deep breath. The shore gave off a green fragrance.

He imitated swimmers, spread his arms, fluttered his feet. He began laughing and, as though astonished by his own voice, put his clothes back on in silence.

Jean walked to the village, opened the door of his house. He lay his hand on Thomas's forehead—the boy was sleeping downstairs. He listened to Michel's slow breathing. Then he climbed the oak stairs to his bedroom. The warm wood felt good under his feet. He opened the door and stopped in the middle of the room. He closed his eyes, listening. He made out Lise's breathing. He dared not move, lest he disturb that slow rhythm. Without opening his eyes, Jean undressed and groped for the bed. He lifted the old quilt and slipped into his place, still there, unchanged. It was cold. Jean smothered a burst of laughter. In silence, a little ashamed, he thought of Lise's warm body.

He lay close to her though she did not make a sound. She was still asleep, but soon opened her eyes. Jean stared at her calm face; he ran a finger down her cheek. He quickly pulled away his hand, which winter had sheathed in stone. Lise opened her lips; Jean sank into them.

When they woke, Lise caressed her husband's beard and said: "Jacques de Saint-Muens died. Do you remember him?"

He nodded. Lise continued: "There are no more grapes on the vines. The leaves are like old women's hands. The wine is poisoned." She slowly passed her hand through Jean's rumpled hair.

"There's a name for the sick vines. They call it phylloxera. I take in washing to make ends meet."

"And the boys?"

"They're fine; I read them your letters. And now you're here."

Jean leaned over Lise; she was naked. He loved her pale eyes. He stood up and walked toward the vineyards.

3

A few years earlier, the Marquise de Saint-Muens had brought her husband some American grape-stocks. She traveled a good deal. So much commotion annoyed Jacques de Saint-Muens. Nowhere pleased him except his property in the Lot. He liked the way the mornings came alive. He loved the giant shadows on the walls, near the chimney. His wife was afraid of them. She preferred staying in Paris.

When his wife came back from America, the marquis barely had time to kiss her forehead: she told everyone about her discoveries.

Jacques de Saint-Muens planted the vine-stocks, the American ones with ochre patches. From his house, he could watch the new vines. He stayed in the Lot all winter long. Evenings, by candle-light, he drew a midnight-blue label: Château Saint-Muens—Amériques—1874. He was excited: a midnight-blue label! He lay a thick book on the walnut table, leafed through a few pages. He was reading Pascal. He daydreamed, imagining the redness of his wine. He sketched the full, round grapes.

Then it was spring.

The sun appeared, and the marquis came out each morning to examine his American vine-stocks. He invited his neighbors. They tasted a few grapes, sucking the skins. They sipped. The sour grapes made their mouths water. They chewed, they spat. The flavor thickened.

Jacques de Saint-Muens was satisfied: this would be a great wine.

The fine weather had wakened the vines. Weeds grew up between the vine-stocks. The clusters grew heavy. The American grapes were reddish ovals: as if they were swollen with blood.

Time passed. A deep sadness overcame the marquis. The midnight-blue label vanished. Jacques de Saint-Muens was depressed about it. He tasted his new grapes and began to worry: the sweetness had disappeared. Tiny wrinkles striped the grape skins. Slowly the leaves withered, burned by the wind.

The disease spread to all the plants in the marquis's vineyard. Jacques de Saint-Muens fell silent. He would have liked his wife to be with him.

He resigned himself to burning his vines in order to retard the contagion. The scorched vine-stocks produced a bitter smoke which swept over the hillsides. Apprehensive, people came to see the effects of the disease. Then they reassured one another: American grapes! What an idea!

One evening, the marquis turned a hunting rifle on his dry face.

About this same time, Pierre Larousse wrote in his *Grand Dictionnaire universel du xixe siècle:* "There are still a number of obscure or completely unknown aspects of the history of phylloxera, such as: the duration of the animal's life, the duration of the period *in ovo,* and the interval separating the molts." And he continued: "When the patch or spot appears at some point on the plant, it is frequently too late to take any measures, the parasite already occupies enormous areas. This is the latent state of the disease, a deceptive and deadly state because it lulls the henceforth ruined viticulturalist into a fatal state of repose."

Near the marquis's estates, no vines resisted. The disease spread to the Lot; the men lost their work.

At Saint-Cirq-Lapopie, people decided to try their luck elsewhere.

When Jean Mardet returned from the front, the fathers of families gathered in the mayor's house. Summer had come; feelings ran high. Two bottles from old times were opened. Each man drank with respect. On the big table, Ramesain spread out a planisphere borrowed from the schoolteacher. Its title was: *Scale Map of the World in Relief*. Altitude was indicated in all the colors of the rainbow; the continents formed huge multicolored bubbles. The Arctic was white, a world of ice. The Antarctic and its vague contours were chestnut. France was tiny, and spring green.

Jean Mardet thought of Lise, of his two children.

Everyone held his breath. A handkerchief was tied around the eyes of the younger boy. He groped his way around the room, until one hand brushed the unfolded map. Then he pointed his finger toward a green patch to the west: Argentina.

4

Once there, Jean Mardet got work as a stevedore. He lived far from his companions, on the harbor of Buenos Ayres. He never seemed to sleep. Days, he carried huge bundles on his shoulders. Late in the tepid evenings, Jean shared his meal with the silent Argentinians. He walked all over Buenos Ayres, humming in the alleys under a pale sky. Mornings, they found him sound asleep in a pile of rope.

Every month, he sent Lise a thick envelope of banknotes; he never wrote. He imagined Thomas and Michel running across the *causse*. He thought about Lise: she must have been expecting a few lines. She went on washing herself with a big sponge, in an icy basin.

When his friends suggested he add a word to their letters, Jean would refuse.

The months passed. Jean Mardet remained silent.

He opened himself to the sun. He let his beard grow, a pirate's beard. He changed jobs and became a bartender in the city. He spoke only French, but he knew all there was to know about the different kinds of alcohol. He knew their names, their features. He invented wonderful drinks, daydreaming all day long. Nights, he mixed cocktails that made you forget. Almost immediately he became famous for his blue or green creations. People said he had the ocean in his eyes. Jean Mardet loved Buenos Ayres.

He grew rich.

During the same period, the little troop from Saint-Cirq-Lapopie decided to return. The men left Argentina with their minds filled with memories, but their pockets empty.

Jean stayed. Each month he sent money. Lise waited. She kept her hopes up, and watched the road through the hills; she reread the address on the heavy envelopes.

Her husband never again gave a sign of life. After a few months, Lise went back to her mother's, at Puymirol. She wept. In Saint-Cirq-Lapopie, the young woman who had made men dream was missed for a long time.

Those who had come back decided to say nothing about Jean's new life. It was better that way. His wife and children were waiting for him: they wouldn't understand his silence. The adventurer was forgotten.

In Buenos Ayres, Jean Mardet remarried—a former dancer, Anna, who gave him a child. She would play for the two of them on a little stringed instrument.

Jean loved those dry harmonies and their changing rhythms. His gaze disappeared over the bright-colored roofs of the city.

He nibbled on a petal which slipped between his teeth, stuck to his palate. His tongue caressed a sour velvet; the flower was bitter. He remembered the Fort of Joux.

Jean bought stills and set to work. He shut himself up in his rooms for several days. Then he quit his job. He opened a little bar where he served absinthe.

People came from everywhere to taste the liquor. Jean stumbled down from the hills with his arms full of gentians and sanicles. He sold flasks of absinthe which would distill joy: wormwood was a sailor's dream.

Jean adopted the slogan of the cafés of Pontarlier: "When in doubt, absinthe yourself!" and he would laugh. He invited his friends, and together they would play cards all night.

At dawn he and Anna would find themselves alone; she would sing under her breath. They would dance for a moment.

She had a good figure, and she was a silent woman. Jean caressed his wife's hips and wept. She kneaded his shoulders; he went off to take a dip in the sea.

Then Jean Mardet left Argentina. He left a family there, a few white walls, two or three bulbs of wormwood.

He saw New York, already straining toward the sky. His ship set sail for Le Havre. In Buenos Ayres, no more was said about the mysteries of absinthe.

THE PATH TO JOSÉ'S

1

To reach the place where José lived, you had to walk through the brush of the *garrigue*. A strange progress toward dreams, our heavy steps through the fields. Sometimes we had to stop, stooping under the heat of the earth.

We would set out at dawn. José lived alone a few leagues from the village. After an hour, we came out onto a chalk promontory, from which the hills stretched as far as you could see. The wind made the women wearing wool shiver.

I was five years old. I still remember Marie, who hugged me close to her. I think she was cold too on those mornings. We dreamed among the hills which the sun would waken later on.

Years afterward, I still hear my parents breathing heavily on their way through that rugged beauty.

We would take "José's path." That was what that stony ascent was called, until the spring of 1915. People who lived in those hills also climbed up to the steep summit. During this rather shame-faced expedition, certain links were created among the climbers. People would give a start, sometimes, at a turn in the path; would smile with that knowing look which intrigues the gendarmes.

Afterward, I wanted to see José's cabin again. For a long time I looked for it without finding a trace of that mysterious path. Silence had fallen around the distiller of the hills.

One morning, I questioned Mailledot, the gendarme, who observed me closely, then went away without saying a word, his hand thrust into his shoulder belt. That departure made me think of José as some kind of wonderful magician. Everyone who had known him loved him as much as I did.

The various aromas of the thorn bushes were intoxicating; we climbed Indian-file, like a column of conspirators, stumbling over invisible roots. The sun rose slowly, and a murky heat began at the horizon. Marie's ample breasts spread an inexpressible moisture over my face.

We knew, halfway up, a secret place to drink when we were thirsty. One day I surprised an animal there—a creature with silvery fur: old women in the village told me it must have been a *boufoin*, a roe deer of the *garrigue*.

A thread of light seemed to bubble up out of the stone, then vanished among the briars. Somewhere in the underbrush it would reappear. Marie baptized it *the magic spring,* so fascinated was she by this icy thread of life which dried on her lips.

We had to be on our way. The climb took us beyond the burning gorges. We emerged from our numbness, borne skyward. The sun was white. All of us were sweating under our straw hats.

We stared into the distance. People said you could see the sea from here, in the autumn. My mother, who was from the region, named the hills for us, sounding rather formal. That was the Madre, to the south, and the Moine, opposite. The landscape became familiar to me. My father would carry me on his shoulders. I pinched his ears, laughing. He would point out Paris, America.

One day my father, usually so silent, pointed into the void: "Look, the sea!"

He was almost shouting. The mist undulated near the blue. We waited. Since the bright water remained invisible, he apologized, and we went on climbing.

Could you really see the sea from such a distance? I still don't know. Myself, divining a presence beyond that dry blue line, I imagined I could make it out, and I understand how, drunk with thirst, approaching the place where José lived, you could entertain this penetrating dream.

2

Of all the happy moments of the excursion, I preferred the return to the village. After several hours with José, we would go back. A silent peace bathed the hills. The approach of darkness drowned the *garrigue* in a tepid sky.

The heat had vanished; we were shivering. My mother covered me with a shawl. Our steps grated. The way down was a series of dreams.

Silence surrounded us. I was half-asleep. Finally the house lights appeared at the bottom of the hill. I returned, dazed, to the bedroom Marie shared with me.

She slept in the big bed, her face buried under the sheets. All I could see was her black hair, and the hillock made by her feet.

I lay down on my bed and thought about José, about our climb up through the *garrigue*. Marie yawned over and over; she was falling back to sleep. If only she would talk to me!

I listened to the night. The moon appeared behind the curtains, silhouetting the furniture in the room; a pale shadow fell across the floor.

I wanted to fall asleep too: I tried breathing steadily. Suddenly I couldn't hear Marie anymore. Anxious, I got up and tiptoed over to where she lay. I lifted the sheet: Marie's face was bright. Her right nostril trembled. I stifled a giggle and returned to my own bed.

My father came to our door. I stopped moving then, and fell asleep without making a sound.

In the morning, Marie thought she was awake before me. She insisted on silence. I heard a rustling noise, the white sheets were moving. Marie was moving around the bed, her black hair mussed. I squinted and held my breath. She was wearing a long white night-gown. She opened the curtains and set a tin basin on a stool. The floor creaked. She left the room and returned, holding a pitcher of water. Then she washed.

She scrubbed her arms enthusiastically. More than once she spilled the water and swore. Her body woke gradually in the morning. I opened my eyes wide: Marie was beautiful. She rinsed herself off slowly, tired. She combed her hair like a schoolgirl. It had become tangled during the night. She dressed; a delicate linen covered her back. Sunlight filled the room.

One day, Marie came over to my bed and sat down on it. I pretended to be asleep; she looked at me without speaking. I forced myself not to think.

She stayed; soon it seemed as if she had been there forever. What was she thinking? I felt her weight on the sheets. Finally, unable to bear it any longer, I burst out laughing. Marie gave a start. I smothered my laughter, which I couldn't stop. She dumped the basin of water over my head. I got dressed and ran outside.

3

One of my favorite games was hunting for crickets. I would listen to their dry song and suppose they were huge insects. I crept through the bushes: I squinted, peering through the thorns without finding anything. Where were they hiding?

Marie would console me. Everywhere, the crickets' song pursued me. Médonin, the big absinthe-drinker of La Cadière, explained that I would never be able to catch a cricket. That was how it was; you could only guess their presence.

One morning, I found Médonin sitting in front of the house. He had moved a table out of the shed and was sitting in front of a black box I had never seen before. I came over to him. Without a word, he pointed to the chair opposite his. Intimidated, I sat down. I could see that Médonin was trembling. He unfolded the wooden object, which became a squared board.

Médonin had a strange expression. He taught me the devious rules of checkers. After that, I played the game with my father. He would ponder a long while: I stumbled over my stool and lost each time.

With Marie, I cheated to let her win: she would smile.

At the summer's end, a tepid rain fell now and then. I waited behind the windows. An ample fragrance rose from the earth.

Our house was made of gray stone and had no name. Its roof was low and sloped over a square framework; thick walls kept things cool. The windows were narrow; each room had its own.

My bedroom was very plain. On one wall I had tacked up a print: "Arrival in New York." It showed the mist rising over a busy harbor, crisscrossed with steamships.

In my bedroom there were only our two beds, and my school desk near the one window.

Sometimes I toiled over my pastel-covered workbooks, but I liked getting out of the house. I would dash down the stairs, skipping two, three, even four steps at a time. Marie would follow me down a dark corridor which opened, downstairs, into a big room where the family meals were eaten. The ochre tiles clattered under our steps. One door opened onto the fields. A stony path led down to the village.

The house had its secrets. In my parents' room, the bed was enormous. At the end of the hallway, opposite the stairs, was a little attic I never went into: the heat was terrible up there in the summer. I loved our house without ever really knowing it very well.

One afternoon when I was about nine, I lit a fire between two stones; over it I set a basin into which I had squeezed some fruit, and then took a carafe from the dresser in the big room. Into my preparation I poured the liquor from which a harsh smell escaped. I was imitating José's gestures.

I filled a flask with this transparent brew and tasted it. It was sweet. I was more surprised than disgusted: how mysterious! I dreamed over my carafe.

When we climbed up to José's, I dared not ask questions.

On the way back, I hid my absinthe under Marie's bed, where I forgot all about it.

4

"José's called José: nothing else."

That was his answer. José had no surname. His past life was a mystery. Médonin explained that José was a diminutive of Joseph. This nickname was popular in Provence. José also meant *fada,* a simpleton.

He was as round as an oak barrel. A beard covered most of his face, so that all you could see was his eyes; it looked like a kind of artificial hemp. His hands were long and strong, his paunch swayed almost gracefully. People said that José could find his way in the dark the way owls do.

One evening, I surprised him gazing out over the valley.

"Good evening, José," I said timidly.

"Evening, *petiot.*"

I buried my hand in his. Night brought us remote echoes. The rocky spine beyond Le Moine had disappeared.

"José," I asked, "what are you looking at?"

He made no answer, only swayed a little. A glow appeared just below the horizon. Suddenly the huge body beside me shuddered, and José said: "I'm watching the night with you, *petiot*."

I could see nothing, but I nodded in silence.

José dressed very simply: canvas trousers, a wide shirt. He wore tanned leather clogs and walked with his feet wide apart. When he came down the path through the bushes, behind his cabin, he was a giant, all red and brown. The dust rose under his feet. José would smile at me and set down his bundle; I ran to him. Fingers between his lips, he whistled for a long time. A shrill sound. We laughed and walked together toward his cabin.

People said that José spoke a remarkable French. He spiced his words with unexpected accents, and called me *petiot*. He had traveled a lot. I think he liked silence best of all. He stayed out in the *garrigue* for hours on end, playing with a stone. I imitated him: I would sit down and finger a round stone. Like José, I was waiting.

Once my father told me that the distiller who lived in the hills didn't know how to write. I was amazed, and annoyed. José knew everything, and he couldn't write? I thought of my own workbooks in which I was laboriously calligraphing the capital letters.

I saw José among the bulbs where the absinthe was growing: a magician. Suddenly I was overcome with doubts. Didn't he have those old recipe books he was always studying so attentively? Didn't he work out the formulas of his liquors? Could José be able to read but not write? A peculiar student!

I'm convinced this was the case. Alone in his laboratory, José would talk to himself. I didn't understand him.

"Jose, what did you say?"

"Nothing, *petiot*. I'm reciting."

His erudition disturbed the people who lived in the hills; José liked hiding the truth. His cabin had a strange name on it: *Fugit amor.*

5

Marie was the only one who had mixed feelings about him. She didn't enjoy our expeditions to the cabin above La Cadière. On those days, she grumbled all the way there.

She was twenty-four years old. Her dark hair was long. Marie's beauty was so complete that her clothes did nothing to conceal it.

On the days we climbed up to José's, Marie dressed slowly. The sun was just rising. She would button her white cotton blouse. I saw her hands stretching the worn cloth over her hips.

Marie took care of me. That way she spared herself harder jobs. I was a peaceful child; she would rather make faces at me than wash the sloping windows of the big room downstairs.

Marie detested absinthe. One day my mother had given her a tiny drop of liquor on a lump of sugar. Marie seemed hesitant. Then she sucked the sugar, alert to the sensations the absinthe might awaken in her. My father was reading, not paying attention. Nothing happened.

"I feel normal, Madame," was all she said.

"Pay attention, Marie, *it's absinthe,*" my father remarked. "Or just listen." He turned a few pages, put on his glasses, and began reading in a low voice:

Believe in love, believe in spring,
after all you are twenty,
and a woman merely passing

your café table has shown you
with a certain intention
six inches of white stocking . . .

Say you are walking arm in arm
or running together beneath
the blue arch of heaven . . .

My mother remained silent. My father turned the page. Marie raised
her hand to her throat: she was choking. She collapsed. My father
quickly slid his thumb between her teeth: there was no danger.

My mother came over to Marie; she pushed my father aside.

Marie slept for several hours. When she awoke, she told us her
astonishing dreams. My mother forbade her to taste absinthe ever
again.

Later on, I found the rest of the poem my father was reading
that day:

Or you lie on the green grass
under the rustling maples,
both of you listening . . .

And it is dark when you come home,
and in the intimacy of the sheets
You fall asleep after an embrace . . .

And all that, my good friends
—I'm only telling you the truth—
is nothing compared to absinthe!

When we were getting close to where José lived, Marie became
hysterical. She would talk feverishly, or else fall silent. The giant
took her hands and kissed her on both cheeks. Marie stammered a
few words. She never went down into the distillery cellars. The
phosphorescent reflections disturbed her.

Just once, Marie had seemed happy in the cabin up above La Cadière; that was the evening when José told us the story of how the tango was born.

6

He liked to collect people around him and tell them his incredible adventures. We would sit in a circle, near the bundles of gentian. The afternoon was ending. The vapors from the still erased any possibility of common sense in us. A great silence reigned. The space of the room closed in around us; we would dream.

Docilely, we listened. Marie folded her arms like a schoolgirl. My mother, her hair coming loose at the back of her neck, sat up straight, her eyes closed. José's words entered into us, and blossomed there. A flame trembled under the golden flasks. Our little group was bathed in pale reflections.

José began abruptly. He would walk back and forth slowly, not looking at anyone, making sweeping gestures. These were mysterious moments. His voice took on remote intonations: José was declaiming. His words, though, were somehow muffled.

At the age of ten, I heard the story of Aloé for the first time. The distiller told it powerfully. An ashen veil descended over the hills. My mother had gone over to where José was standing and was talking to him in an undertone. We were sitting on the warm tiles. José had begun:

"Long, long ago, there were giants living in faraway lands. They would dance naked; their movements were free and supple. And these gestures attracted women. Patagonia, that was the name of this harsh country. It was at the end of the world, and the soil there was gray.

"No one worked there but only danced, all day long.

"When night fell, the giants would continue. The warm sand vanished into the ocean, beneath the horizon. The giants were dancing to the music of the winds.

"One morning, a young woman no one knew, a stranger with a bright body, arrived in Patagonia. Her breasts were lovely. She danced with the giants who had no desires now save for her; they loved her pale hips, her graceful neck bending beneath her long amber hair. Her name evoked the peaceful winds, the song of pebbles under the receding wave; her name was Aloé.

"The women of Patagonia were jealous of Aloé, and derided her paleness. And what kind of name was that?

"Aloé was a sign dancing on the sea.

"She observed the ocean. In a reflection, she discovered her shoulder reddened by the sun, and she wept. She left, all by herself, and was gone for an entire day. And returned radiant, swathed in a long orange cloth which she had knotted around her loins.

"The women exclaimed: 'Aloé! What have you done to your body now? Why are you hiding it from the sun?' They derided her anew. The giants were astonished to see her like this. During their dances, Aloé's legs made the tango cloth ripple. And Aloé's breast had bronzed under the sun.

"The Patagonian giants were forgetting their own women and dreamed only of Aloé."

José fell silent, stretched out one hand. We hung on his every word. Provence and Argentina were one and the same. No one moved. José continued:

"One night, Aloé disappeared. They searched for the young woman all night long. At dawn, her body was discovered in the sea. The gray water was licking her legs, spread wide apart. The tango skirt was pushed high above her knees.

"The jealous women had killed Aloé. No one dared approach

the body, troubled as they all were by desire. The giants saw Aloé's nakedness, and wept.

"Fire devastated Patagonia: that was the end of such dancing, delicious as it had been.

"All that remained, half in the sea, was the lovely dancer's body, no longer covered by the tango cloth.

"That flesh gradually became land. Aloé turned to sand, and gave birth to the shore of Buenos Ayres.

"Today, the women of that place still wear such cloth, tango cloth which they raise in the passing winds.

"In the language of the poets, *tango* means orange."

7

When José had finished this tale, there was a long silence. My father stared at the potbellied still. My mother would not speak. Aloé had secretly troubled them. Marie's face was aflame.

I was dazzled by this elliptical visit of the universe.

We would have liked to extend those moments enveloped by the darkness. The words blurred. Only those dances remained, and José's voice.

I didn't do much reading; such tales told me of the beauty of the world.

I was exhausted. My father rocked back and forth in the warm evening air, his thin hands on his knees. I dared not come close to him.

He put his glasses back on and smiled at me, embarrassed. Then José burst out in a terrible laugh which made us all jump, embarrassed: it was time to go home.

ABSINTHE

1

One morning when I had awakened early, Marie was no longer there. The sheets, usually rumpled, were folded on the edge of her bed. The night before, Marie had been there—I still saw her heavy shape in the darkened air.

She had vanished during the night; I learned that she was to be married. Aloé had fled from the bedroom where I would henceforth be alone.

To console me, it was decided that we would go up to José's cabin. Silently, my mother walked ahead; my father, to one side, clasped his hands behind his back. Deep in my throat, I choked back my long sobs.

The valley was a scorching basin.

That day when a story had lied, I discovered absinthe. I was nine years old.

José embraced me. I would have liked to hide my tears. He simply told me: "Suck the sugar, *petiot.*"

And he handed me a tiny white cube which absinthe was turning green. I took it from him, uneasy. It felt harmless enough. The sugar didn't crumble between my fingers; it was smooth, fragile, both sustained and decomposed by its bitter pallor.

I had seen my parents drown their sugar in coffee, which had diluted its whiteness. Absinthe, on the contrary, gave the sugar a strong coloration. The bitter flavor made my eyes water.

Their faces were lowered toward me. They seemed to be telling me: "Go on, you'll see how amazing it is!"

Médonin, who was there too, stared at me strangely. I brought the sugar to my lips. The white pebble seemed quite ordinary. Forgetting my anxiety, I set it on my tongue. I waited. Tiny grains came loose, liberating within me a transparent essence. I savored my own saliva, which had turned bitter in my mouth. The mysterious mixture rinsed my throat. Absinthe blazoned its colors: an exciting sweetness drowned my mind.

I could not think anymore. A vague fear came over me. It vanished, covered with sand. I felt that I, too, had dissolved. My soul was velvet. I was infinitely distant. Absorbed by the nascent drug, I was a vermilion flake. My senses reacted to every sound. My hands trembled. From a great distance I could hear someone asking anxiously: "Do you think he's feeling something?"

I closed my eyes. I stood stock still. The furniture shifted position: there was a wave of color. José was talking to me. I held my hand out, into the void.

My eyes were burning. I could no longer see objects except by the light of which they were an echo. I tried to sit on a chair. They made me lie down. I didn't speak a word. A world opened up inside me. I was calm. I saw Marie, quite close. We were playing checkers, and the colors were extraordinarily vivid. My father's huge hands were caressing my forehead. I breathed very slowly; my breath was a wind. I was deliciously exhausted.

The fainting fit had been momentary. When I stood up, dazed, I staggered. My father was holding my right hand. I searched within myself for the causes of the mystery. Absinthe had seized me and flung me into this dream. I decided to go back to José's and try to understand. That night, I listened carefully to the distiller, seeking in his stories the key to the wormwood gates.

I couldn't describe that dream. The absinthe sugar was an avalanche. That night, I went to bed alone. I thought about my troubled nights; I saw Marie wake up in her bed, transparent. I heard the clear water flowing in the tin basin.

2

I returned frequently to the giant of the hills, who raised me in his hands, to heaven itself. The cabin was built of dark stones; you reached it by following a path overgrown with high grass.

The ground floor seemed uninhabited; one or two pieces of furniture were flung here and there. Running my hand over a dusty table, I touched some books bound in thick leather. They seemed to be encyclopedias of spells; the pages were of some ancient substance. I leafed through them slowly, deciphering a few words. I unfolded a white sheet on which was written:

Slowly let your your hand increase
The green infusion. Then add more
Water, keeping your hand high. Stop
Once you see the liquor is clear enough.

I recognized my father's handwriting and set the book down again.

When José was used to my presence, I saw him consult one of those books. "Come over here, *petiot*." That was more than I had hoped for: my mother's glances had made José behave very cautiously. The book was embellished with old illuminations. I followed José's finger down the page, along the arabesques.

Later on, when the distiller had vanished into the hills, I searched in vain for those books of wonder. I found only one of them, a duodecimo; those brightly illustrated writings had lost their mystery. The formulas no longer evoked absinthe. But in the days when José spread his vapors through the valley, his books of spells constituted a mysterious summons.

At the rear of that empty room was a door. It looked as if it opened onto the hills; it led to a magical room which José called his "laboratory." I could enter there without permission. I learned the secret word; I stole memories in order to go on dreaming in the *garrigue*.

The door was often ajar, and you could just make out there was a still in there. You went down a few steps into the shadows. The room was lighted by a single candle. It was an old cellar. The light there was subaqueous; there were strange whistles and palpitations. A gust of wind coming from nowhere ran through the row of gas jets, at the mouth of the distillation flasks. A bitter odor took you by the throat: it choked the atmosphere.

Hidden in a corner of the room, some young girls I had never met were desperately pressing rags over their faces; or else, on the third step, they raised their hands to their white-cotton chests. I held my breath: would they stay? I waited for some kind of assurance.

Some of them retreated quickly, others unlaced their bodices and leaned against the cold wall; I grew accustomed to these mysterious excitements.

The demijohns were set on the black dirt floor, from which sparks rose. I could make out the alchemist's retorts, recognize the stages of the distillation. I would lay my cheek against the warm flasks: José was tiny and green.

The cellar was a magical site where your senses remained always alert. It was a feast for the ear, caressed by hisses. My parents allowed me to visit José on my own: I became accustomed to doing so. Every day I would climb the hill of La Cadière.

The distiller had grown used to my presence. He worked without paying any attention to me. He seemed to project an extraordinary joy.

The day passed; I would follow José.

Stiff in every limb, I staggered home through the *garrigue*. My mind enchanted by new tales, I inhaled the warm evening air.

3

On the occasion of these visits of mine to José's cabin, I made a discovery: a secret.

The distiller opened a wooden crate and took two crystal carafes out of it. At first their colors looked very much alike. The first one José showed me was a deep green. In the light, tiny particles fluttered in that sea. Without a word, José set it back down on its straw bed.

The other carafe was the dry green of the late summer sky. I stood on the doorstep: this one was absinthe mixed with gold. José was standing behind me. Gently, he took the carafe out of my hands, raised it very high, and through the transparent glass the sky turned to copper. The distiller smiled at me.

"You see, *petiot,* there are two absinthes. That's a secret: keep it to yourself. You won't find it in any book. This gold carafe contains the absinthe called *gentiana lutea.*"

José stared hard at the flask, turning it round and round. The liquid rose and fell, spread, sloshed against the cork. Tiny bubbles pierced the gold. José continued: "It's a mixture of gentian, anise, fennel, and hyssop. For this one, I don't use the usual weights. It's a dangerous absinthe: never drink it!"

He kept this treasure in his hand: "You know what this other carafe is—the absinthe of the trade. Never repeat this. And never taste the *gentiana lutea.*"

José had a great respect for the liquors. He took me out into the *garrigue,* far beyond his cabin. I had never followed this mountain path. We climbed up without a word. José had brought the golden carafe.

Soon the slope leveled off; we came out onto a narrow white plateau. We walked ahead: Provence slumbered before us. I could barely distinguish the rock formations from the hidden hamlets. La Cadière had vanished from sight. With a huge effort, José flung the carafe away: it broke into a luminous rain.

He distilled only the absinthe called *artemisia absinthium,* a pure liquor with which he mixed a few twigs of fennel.

José added flavors to his liquors—sage, mint. He also possessed various little accessories for the ladies, who would sit on a worn bench, overlooking the valley. Then I would bring José the absinthe spoons: these were silver, with lozenge-shaped perforations. He would take one and fasten it above a tall glass. He set a lump of sugar in the bowl of the spoon. From very high above it, he poured a warmed thread of absinthe.

At first the sugar remained white. The absinthe spread in bitter channels. Then, from inside, an emerald star appeared. It was a dream pebble which the delicate ladies put under their tongues.

Those times were fun. My father would often tell us about Paris: Monsieur Eiffel's tower and its vertigo, the wonderful alignments of the Right Bank, the glass roofs of the Petit Palais. My mother folded her arms; she watched my father, smiling. I imagined the cafés of the Grand Boulevards which served an impure absinthe. In the Place de l'Opéra, automobiles made by Panhard & Levassor would pass the lordly fiacres.

I would watch the effects of the absinthe on people drinking it for the first time. How strange it was, seeing these beings overwhelmed from within.

Their senses would stretch, joyously deploying this soaring poison. The sugar vanished under the taste buds. And absinthe blossomed within the soul, like a flower. Unlike other alcohols, it was pure pleasure. It developed the imagination, and offered a spiritual depth to dreams.

4

The fires never went out under José's flasks. At night, strange liquors seethed, evaporated. They struggled through the galvanized copper retorts before condensing as alcoholic spirits.

The bundles of gentian were drying on the cellar ceilings. They scattered a thick dust. These plants had been picked by José. Their stems were a silky, silvery green. The leaves were gray above, white underneath. For weeks on end, they dried in the dark. When José's knife slit the rough canvas sacks, a silent bomb pierced the cellar: a mass of twigs burst free, then fell back in a dry rain.

This absinthe dust would then macerate in clear water which José would bring back in barrels from the mountain. I believe he knew a hidden spring where the water spurted directly out of the rock. Over a constant fire, the dust dissolved; the liquid turned the color of straw.

This stage of the preparation always disappointed me. A harsh-colored liquid covered the sides of the flasks, unable to rise. Golden splinters mounted toward the open mouthpiece, where they exploded in a fine shower. The copper and glass flasks were held in wooden trays. What would Marie have thought of all this beauty? Would she have shuddered, startled?

José observed his labors with a distant gaze. The gentian petals were gradually consumed in a "three-six" brandy. The distiller used eighty-gram brass weights. The proportions of the absinthe were mysterious.

Like those Indian poisons of which a single drop is lethal, the pure wormwood was dissolved in an ordinary alcohol which was gradually impregnated with bitterness. In José's hands, it became an impeccable essence.

The operation was known as *coloration*. It was like the meeting of a characterless lover and a marvelous woman—a love which would have consumed the weakling. José mixed the liquids with a sweeping gesture. It was this movement which gave the absinthe its beauty. Beside the enormous flasks in which the gentian dust macerated, these lidless cauldrons were nothing; for dreams, there had to be explosions, a golden rain.

The liquor was born of the coloration. The essence created had a terrible odor and made my eyes water. José used it to drive off the insects attracted by the lights of the laboratory.

José would then filter this thick liquid through a canvas sieve. Tiny granules remained caught at the bottom. I kept them in a little tin box, an inestimable treasure. By daylight, I lifted the lid, which advertised a brand of vanilla cookies. I would caress the fine powder. Once I flung a handful of it into the hills. The grains shimmered for a second.

The distiller finally combined the essence and the coloration. Like oil and water, they ignored each other. Then, over the flames, the two voices of absinthe united. A great heat reigned in the cellars. The twin flasks were linked by a coiled condenser. I saw the birth of the absinthe: the two effervescences corresponded. The gases mingled. A dense green invaded the flasks whose bases had turned red.

Through a divided neck a thread of steam escaped, which José assured me was very important. This was an opaque residue which, in escaping, colored the absinthe. It was born with the loss of its soul.

Hours went by. Darkness crept up the hills. The flasks illumined the laboratory with a faint green glow.

5

The escaping effluence was known as *the angels' share.*

One evening, José fastened a glass plate near the mouth of the flask. A sort of snow formed like hoarfrost, a crystalline sugar: absinthe vapor. There was a scientific explanation for this sublimation in reverse. It set me dreaming: that burning powder which dissolved into air—was it not the living part of the absinthe? *The angels' share:* the name left no doubt. The wormwood lived by that disappearance.

José taught me that the pale absinthe would be too severe for our organism. I was disappointed. The principle of the alcohol was that peculiar powder one never saw in the carafes.

Days went by. I stayed, fascinated by that delicate ebullition. Close to the coiled condenser floated the spirit's essence.

I believe that my soul, too, was consumed by the absinthe. To each of us, the liquor offered a hope of forgetting oneself in a marvelous, absent world.

A final operation was necessary for the absinthe to exist. It had to circulate for hours on end in glass coils. I scorned this stage of the distilling process, which seemed pointless to me. Once the coloration was over, and the filtering, and the maceration, what was the use of these instruments? I hadn't the slightest idea. José would watch these moments closely. I waited for a sign, a palpitation; in vain.

I could not imagine, without proofs, that this was a decisive stage. It had no name and performed no visible transformation on the absinthe. It took the memory of the preceding moments, the vigilance of my enormous friend, for my mind to waken.

A pewter spigot closed the still. Suddenly a spitting was perceptible; a little dust settled. I held my breath. The absinthe we were waiting for flowed out. I collected this ocean-green lava in a bottle. It was simple, after all.

6

After the Second World War, I passed through Pontarlier. All day I waited for the Geneva train. I saw the monumental gate, the grand avenue which divided the town. On each side of the avenue, I imagined places where people used to drink absinthe: there was nothing left but shops, groceries, hardware stores.

The Avenue de la République led to the plains of the Cluse. A friend accompanied me there; it was springtime. The mountain flowed down to our feet, brimming over. We walked in silence, between the steep walls of stone.

I returned alone toward town. In a large bookstore, I bought a work by some local historian: *Pontarlier, capitale de l'absinthe*. A little later, I sat down on a café terrace to leaf through those bright-colored pages. I read the solemn explanations concerning absinthe. I thought of José.

To pass the time, I went to the town library, where I consulted an encyclopedia. I turned to the article "Absinthe." I copied out formulas. I studied the typology of spoons, the collections of flasks and bottles. I learned the story of the Franc-Comtois doctor Pierre Ordinaire.

I discovered the various trade names of the absinthe spoons: Cailar et Bayard, Auzolle, and many others too.

The processes described in these reference works were those of the great distilleries of the period and bore no resemblance to what José had been doing in his cabin. I returned to the site of the ancient house of Pernod Fils, just east of Pontarlier. Nothing was left but a huge shed in the middle of a peaceful field.

I learned that an *absinthier* is a man who runs after girls, and that *absinthe* still signified, in the last century, "bitter displeasure."

The liquor was nothing but a word. At the end of the day, I bought a newspaper and some cigarettes. Then I went back to the melancholy Pontarlier station, where a red and green Micheline railroad car was waiting.

So how am I to describe what no longer exists? Who will tell the life story of the forbidden alcohol?

THE GREAT
INVESTIGATIONS

1

By October, Provence was wrapped in gray. Evenings set in early. The stones of the path were blue; their shapes mingled. Shadows fell over the valley. Autumn was a silent pacification.

It was the year 1911. I was coming from José's, walking fast. Halfway down, a clanking of spurs and bridle almost frightened me: two riders, walking alongside their horses. They seemed tired. Such encounters were rare in these hills. The two men were wearing uniforms: gendarmes. One of them pointed at his kepi: "Hey there, boy, do you know where Monsieur José's cabin is?"

That name sounded funny: *Monsieur José*. I smiled. Then, when I showed them the steep path, they sighed.

I turned toward the peak: their silhouettes blurred in the darkness.

In the village I learned that an investigation was under way concerning "liquors, alcohols, and distillery products." Absinthe constituted the object of special attention.

José's cabin did not appear on any map of the region. The two gendarmes questioned the villagers: answers were vague. Pursued by rumors, they climbed up toward the hills. Was that the end of absinthe? Would José be arrested? People gossiped in the cafés, around the square. The Anti-alcoholism Committee of the Chamber of Commerce was powerful; a vague anxiety seized the inhabitants of La Cadière.

Soon, however, people began to smile. They wished the investigators good luck! Did they want to interrogate José, the great distiller? Make him talk about absinthe? Let them try! José would know how to welcome them. And the village was all exaggerated nods, smiles, winks. People alluded to absinthe as though it were a great secret.

The next morning, we saw the two gendarmes coming back down: they were pale. Their uniforms were covered with dust. In the village streets, their horses clattered over the cobblestones and sounded anything but military.

Very soon, we learned about the day Chief Sergeant Rouillet and Sergeant Meunot had spent. These gentlemen from the city knew very little about absinthe. And nothing of Provençal asperities.

Riding uphill had been exhausting. The riders finally saw José's cabin. The distiller was surprised to see them. He shook hands with his intimidated visitors and offered them a glass. The gendarmes refused authoritatively: tired, but on duty.

Their orders were quite clear: to question José about his methods of distillation and to find out who the man was. As evening fell, the three men went down into the cellar together, remaining there a good part of the night. Slow vapors escaped from the still. The gendarmes took a seat; the investigation began. Rouillet asked long questions. The distiller frowned, then answered, walking back and forth among the flasks.

The chief sergeant kept wiping his forehead. He soon began having a very bad headache. Meunot was worried for his superior, and for himself as well: the hissing noises in the cellar, Monsieur José's stern face disturbed him. The two gendarmes asked to leave the laboratory.

Rouillet and Meunot took off their kepis; they took a few steps on the stony path. José brought them two glasses of cold water. They sat in silence. The landscape was motionless, bright. The investigators breathed slowly. José watched them.

After a few moments, Rouillet stood up and ordered his sergeant to protect his nose and mouth. Both men attched moist handker-chiefs to their faces.

José preceded them into the cellar, where the questions resumed. The gendarmes, henceforth, worked without difficulty. They confiscated two small vials of absinthe, inspected the bundles of petals. Between his fingers, Meunot rolled the grains in the bottom of the sieve. They watched the coloration. Everything was scrupulously set down in a notebook.

The dawn came. Handshakes. The gendarmes removed their robbers' bandannas and with some hesitation refused a glass of absinthe. They rode down toward La Cadière.

2

Médonin had taken charge of the story, which he told in his feverish voice to little groups. Was it true? According to my father, he had heard it from José. We never knew.

Chief Sergeant Rouillet and Sergeant Meunot never came back. They had met with several distillers, from Menton to the west of Marseille. Their report was not taken seriously.

The two gendarmes were young men. They described quite precisely the distillation and the dangers of absinthe: they even seemed to have experienced some of its sensations.

Rouillet insisted on the atmosphere of conspiracy that reigned in the hills. Monsieur José concealed himself from the government agents. Absinthe released unhealthy vapors into the air. All this was probable enough, but the report suggested that the two gendarmes had been fascinated by the object of their investigation. Such indifference turning so quickly into passion produced a bad impression in Marseille.

The prefect in charge of transmitting his agents' report to the Chamber's Committee of Public Hygiene took a certain pleasure in leafing through these pages; one copy was kept for the archives, and the original sent to Paris.

Today this scrupulous text can be consulted in the archives of the prefecture of Marseille. It relates in detail the visit to seventeen artisanal distilleries and lingers over the village of La Cadière. It was with great joy that I rediscovered José in these academic pages.

"Sergeant Meunot and I, Chief Sergeant Rouillet, having received orders from the prefect of Marseille to conduct an investigation, proceeded to study in due form the conditions of absinthe fabrication in the cantons of Provence. Following the description of our visit to the seventeen distilleries given below, we hoped to reach a conclusion in the vicinity of the village of La Cadière. There we encountered one Monsieur José, a sinister figure who distills his absinthe in a cabin not far from that village.

"We noted, in the first place, that the fundamental rules of hygiene were not respected in this dark cellar. The flasks, pipettes, and stills are neither cleaned nor disinfected as they should be. With the consequence that there are certain deposits in the liquor.

"Furthermore, the methods employed by Monsieur José are mysterious and do not in any point correspond to the criteria currently applied to distillation. Enormous bundles of petals are drying and rotting in that 'laboratory.' The resulting dust—which common sense would suggest scattering in the valley—is subsequently mingled with all kinds of unknown alcohols. These translucent liquors leak, seethe, evaporate, and stagnate for hours on end. Monsieur José has given whimsical names to what he calls the 'stages' of his work: *sifting, coloration, the angels' share.* The sergeant and myself were alarmed by such frivolity and by such ignorance of the gentian liquor. The flasks of absinthe are neither sealed nor even labeled: only their characteristic green color permits the specialist to distinguish them from a simple brandy.

"Finally, the consumption of absinthe is developing among the population a spirit of rebellion likely to to call into question the public order which we represent. I shall cite as an example the difficulties which Sergeant Meunot and I encountered in our search for the residence of the object of the investigation. The distiller's cabin does not appear on the cadastral survey. It was hidden in the *garrigue,* and we were obliged to interrogate the reticent villagers in order to reach it.

"The information given was anything but reliable. My colleague and I followed a steep path. A young shepherd, finally, brought us to the cabin."

The narrative continued at great length. Médonin appeared in it as a person "devoured by absinthe." The last lines concluded:

"Hence all the evil consequences of this poisonous alcohol, which may be recognized by its phosophorescent greenish tinge. Absinthe has the property of glowing in the dark. This is one of the reasons which provokes its incredible fascination among the people. No doubt it would be advisable, as our investigation emphasizes, to regulate more severely the production of absinthe in the cantons visited."

In Marseille, the keeper of the archives was surprised when I asked to consult this document. She was a pleasant young woman, blond and cheerful. She brought me a volume covered with rice paper in pristine condition. On the last page, a card in a pocket established the history of this text. That was in 1952; the book had been consulted only once before, thirty years previously.

3

In 1906, a parliamentary group was created to oppose alcoholism. Ribot, in the Chamber, sought the prohibition of absinthe.

That same year, five drafts of laws were offered: in the Senate, the Siegfried and Béranger proposals. In the Chamber, the Vaillant, Breton, and Buisson-Guyesse proposals.

In February 1906, Vaillant demanded the prohibition of aromatic wines and liquors. Absinthe was not cited. The text called too many alcohols into question: it was rejected by a wide margin.

Breton, some months later, advocated the definitive prohibition of absinthe. There was some applause. Night had fallen; in the blue shadows of the Chamber floor, the proposal was rejected.

Soon, public opinion proved favorable to a more severe regulation. In Parliament, proposals were made in rapid succession.

In June 1907, Schmidt's text was examined by the Parliamentary Committee on Hygiene. This deputy sought to extend the prohibition to the French colonies; without success.

The Senate in its turn required measures taken against the liquor. At the beginning of 1908 the Lamarzelle proposal was registered.

Four years after it had been formulated, this stringent text was rejected.

The press ridiculed the project, which had circulated from committee to committee. Venton, a journalist on the *Charivari,* wrote at the time: "Four years! Four years! How astonishing that the Larmarzelle proposal, so concerned to preserve public order, so desirous to prohibit absinthe in France for good, limps for years on end through the corridors of the Senate, comes up against closed doors in committee, is lost in the labyrinths of the Upper Chamber, applauded, saluted . . . already forgotten!"

The senatorial committee, on the other hand, approved the Ouvrier text, which prohibited all liquors with a base of thujone. Public opinion was satisfied.

At the same period, Chairman Saunet received the records sent by the prefects of Besançon and Marseille. The committee was called into session. Saunet recommended immediate prohibition of absinthe. Too vague and feverish, his text was relegated to the archives of the Chamber.

In the spring of 1914, Lyautey, resident-general in Morocco, prohibited production, consumption, and possession of absinthe throughout the protectorate. In metropolitan France, questions were asked: had the time come to repudiate wormwood?

At the beginning of the war, Hennion, police prefect of the Seine, officially prohibited the liquor within his department. His example was followed virtually everywhere in France.

These fiscal regulations were followed, in due form, by various decrees and statutes.

The vise was closing.

4

On June 28, 1914, Archduke Franz-Ferdinand, heir to the throne of Austria-Hungary, was assassinated at Sarajevo by a Serbian student. Feelings ran high, and the following month, Austria declared war on Serbia. Russia mobilized thirteen army corps; on August 1, France and Germany ordered general mobilization.

A few days later, Belgium was invaded. Battles broke out in the east: the First and Second French Armies were stopped at Morhange; the German troops were blocked before they reached Nancy. The Great War was beginning.

Early in the morning of August 2, I went to the village and bought the newspaper. The ink stuck to my fingers. An unprecedented headline filled the first page:

WAR

I ran toward our house shouting: "War!—war's been declared!"
No one would believe it.

My mother had heard me shouting. I remember that she came
out onto the doorstep, a bright rag in her hand. When I saw her, I
ran even faster: I stood in front of her and showed her the rumpled,
almost torn newspaper. Gulping, I exclaimed: "It's war!"

I didn't want to cry. My mother thrust the rag into her pocket.
She repeated in a whisper: "War . . ." And said nothing more for a
long time. Her face was shiny. She ran her hand through her hair
and hugged me against her. Some clouds ran together to form a
white horizon.

Each evening, coming home from school, I would read the newspaper. I sat down and unfolded the big pages on the downstairs table.
Head on my hands, I would study the Bulletins from the Front. On
the map where the armies of France and Germany kept shifting position, I discovered the north of the country: the Ardennes, Strasbourg.
I learned illustrious names: Joffre, Franchet d'Esperey, Gallieni.

On September 2, the First German Army was twenty-five kilo-
meters from Paris. I trembled.

My father had not yet left: he was working on the maintenance
and supervision of highway and railroad networks in southern
France.

Summer's end was filled with sunshine.

In the valley of the Ourcq, that September, Gilles Charon was
killed by a bullet through the heart. This was the first inhabitant of
La Cadière carried off by the war. I can still see the women dressed
in black praying in the village church. After the service, we climbed
up the scorching path to the little cemetery. Faces were grim.

Only José still laughed. He never mentioned the battles. He
found me pensive. One evening when I had nothing to say, he told
me about New York:

"All I saw was the harbor. We were coming from Latin America. My ship was leaving for France. Strange gray buildings rose into the sky; the city's horizon was made of steel. Steamships crisscrossed the harbor in all directions. As if in a dream, the ocean took us. Very quickly, New York became a surprisingly fixed point, in the distance."

When I asked him how he had known that city, José looked at me for a moment, but made no answer.

He continued making his absinthe. No one talked about it much in La Cadière.

5

In January 1915, Doctor Dumont, Surgeon General of the Armies, was appointed liaison to the Chamber for questions of public hygiene. After a month, he presented the results of his investigation, as follows:

"Gentlemen, members of the Committee on Hygiene of the Chamber and of the Senate: I submit to you, this February 12, 1915, the reflections you have requested of me concerning the liquor known as absinthe, and its use in France.

"Considered as a holy substance by the medieval empiricists, the alcohol absinthe was long regarded as a remedy for ills of every kind. The absinthe cure was the most frequent treatment of the eighteenth century, along with bleeding: this is a sign.

"This liquor is identified by its extraordinary bitterness. Its methods of fabrication are obscure and numerous. They were already indexed in the recipe books of the Middle Ages.

"Allow me a brief scientific digression. Absinthe is composed of a bitter principle which is mixed with alcohol and other vegetable substances. Twelve percent of this liquor derives from thujone, prohibited by law in 1912, which is absolutely poisonous to the human nervous system. No comment is required: absinthe aggravates tuberculosis, contributes to criminality, and perturbs the understanding of those who give themselves up to it without reservation.

"It is certain that this liquor exerts a great fascination upon the populace, in cities as in the countryside. For the ancients, absinthe suggested health. In these wartime days, it is a source of further disease."

Then, raising his voice, Surgeon General Dumont concluded by demanding the prohibition of the liquor.

"A mind unfamiliar with scientific procedures may be abused by the mysterious coloration of the wormwood, by its harsh odor. For my part, gentlemen, I insist upon recommending—and I am convinced you will understand my position—the definitive prohibition of the fabrication, sale, and circulation of absinthe in France."

Unanimous applause.

6

In the spring of 1915, my father was assigned to the region of Champagne. He took part in the major campaigns of 1916, and participated in the liberation of Douaumont in October, under the high command of General Mangin. His letters were brief, filled with resignation. They always began with: "My wife, my child . . ." My mother would read them to me in a faint voice. I no longer went to buy the newspaper.

I was living alone with my mother.
She would tell me about her childhood, about José's journeys. We would walk for hours on end in the hills; she gathered all kinds of flowers and told me their strange names.

In 1918 my father returned.

We went to meet him at the railroad station in Aix. A very long train came in, clattering past the crowd on the quay. A signalman's whistle pierced the silence. Suddenly I saw my father. He was wearing a uniform. There was a gray bandage on his left leg, and he limped. My mother recognized him and gave me something like a smile. We tried to move forward. The crowd made that impossible. My father came toward us: he had grown thinner.

That evening, we walked calmly through the streets of La Cadière; the sky was bright. The war was over.

INFLUENCES

1

Sometimes, the heat grew stifling in José's laboratory. Everything was silent movement, flight and flow. I made a little sign to the distiller, opened a low door in the rear of the room, and stepped over an earthen threshold. I was then in a sort of shed lit by a vent: a dungeon. The sun entered for six minutes a day. The plank door closed behind me. I sat down on a tiny three-legged stool.

The air was cool; nighttime, it seemed. A strange calm prevailed in there. The walls were covered with a kind of black metal fretwork, on which rested hundreds of flasks. Only the low ceiling was bright.

This was the cellar where the absinthe was kept. I delighted in the motionlessness of the place; and I was amazed by the silence of things.

I tried to recognize the various absinthes. The bottles were transparent, with narrow mouths, sealed with wax. They had no labels. Depending on the time of day, the liquor changed color. Evenings, they seemed to be flint blue, flagons of ether.

There was an infinity of greens down there. José would say, with a laugh: "It's a *jungle*."

I had the feeling of an imperceptible order. I caressed the flasks, the cold metal fretwork that held them. Sometimes I would grab a bottle that slid through my fingers like a crumpled cloth. If it bumped against its shelf, a shrill note sounded. The cellar congealed: the sound gradually faded away.

My hands left a dark trace on the dusty glass. I followed the reflections: a few vermilion streaks near the wax seal. I glanced around at this incredible store. Then I would put the bottle down, afraid of not finding its proper place. I held my breath: order was restored. Dampness had hardened the black soil. The absinthe was waiting in the dark.

2

My mother was born in Provence: she was one of its flowers.

I can see her now, walking with a light step toward José's cabin. She always wore linen dresses, dyed various colors. Sometimes she would hold my hand; hers was cool.

She rarely laughed. Her face was long, filled with silences. After such an interval, her voice faded. But every once in a while, a chance meeting with others affords me the same peace. For a moment I am surprised, then I see my mother turning toward me. She smiles.

When my father and I played checkers, she would sit beside us, leaning her head on her left hand. She followed the game, and now and again would move one of my pieces. Then my father would say, reproachfully: "The boy has to learn, Louise." And would add: "That's cheating!"

He frowned, and my mother, smiling, would tap his hand and answer: "Besides, you'd already lost!"

Then my father would make three kings, one after the other.

Louise: it's an old-fashioned name today. Since I called her Maman, I was always surprised to hear my father call her that.

She would turn toward him, then, slowly. I remember that elegant gesture of her neck, prolonged by her gaze and concluding, so tenderly, on her lips.

My mother took litle pleasure in absinthe; she rarely drank it at all. She preferred listening to José and watching him while he told his stories. I think she would have enjoyed traveling. His words were her wormwood. She was the one who took down José's words in a lined notebook, the kind we used at school. When I opened it, I recognized her careful handwriting. All the stories were there, even the escape of Baïan, the Mongol heroine.

As I used to do in the past, I moved my finger along the words my mother had written. I rediscovered Aloé, and her Argentinian dances: that was her favorite story.

All of which now seems so far away.

At the beginning of the war, my school closed. I would study the dictionary. My mother would choose an unusual word, which I would carefully copy out. Then we would make up its meanings: that was fun. For *déclive* I thought of an exotic fruit. The *déclivier* would be a pale tree with delicate branches. Or else the *déclivier* was a municipal employee, a sort of sewerman. Even today, as I write these words, they emerge under my pen with a certain savor.

My mother would invent all kinds of games. For geography, she shuffled the engravings of the big cities I was to recognize. Gradually, I would take out the ones I had grown familiar with: Paris or London, river cities. But there was Casablanca, Tunis, Hanoi, Rome, Lisbon, Buenos Ayres. These reproductions joined "Arrival in New York" on my bedroom wall.

During the war, one morning, I went to find my mother in her room; I was bored. She was sitting at her dressing table, washing her face. I stood behind her, and she gave me a wink in the mirror. She slowly wiped her face with a rough towel, then ran a brush through her fine hair. That gesture reminded me of Marie. I was daydreaming in front of the mirror. My mother handed me the fragrant brush from which I would pull out the long dark hairs.

My parents died young. I knew them very little. I believe they loved each other. For a long time, they continued their walks in the hills. Then they got sick and died.

3

My father, Claude, came from the north of France: a little village, I don't even know its name. He left school very young to become an apprentice: he learned the surveyor's trade on the highways.

He owned a number of delicate instruments of which he was extremely proud. Sometimes he would let me look through his strange graduated field glasses: the landscape seemed to be distorted by a graph of black threads which measured everything off. He also had some incredible yardsticks. For a little while, he would let me play with his tools, then he put them away in a heavy leather valise.

I loved it when he explained the mysteries of his trade to me. One Sunday, he took us just outside La Cadière on a new road. He stamped on the gray pavement; Louise smiled.

My father's expression became exalted. He thought for a moment. With a piece of chalk, he drew thick layers on the side of the road. Enthusiastically, he explained to me how the road would resist our footsteps; there was the pavement, then under that there was just sand, shale, gravel, pebbles. I looked at the dark road and tried to imagine the series of substances; to no avail. My father, seeing my doubts, went behind a shack. He returned, carrying a metal bar. He took off his jacket, spit on his palms, and began, quite gaily, to take apart the roadway. Pieces flew in all directions.

He smiled at me: "You'll see." Suddenly he stopped: "No, not here! In the center, of course, in the center!"

With a clump of dirt, he filled the hole he had just dug. Then, his legs wide apart, quite methodically, he began pounding the pavement, blow after blow. I was fascinated. My mother approached; she lay one hand on my father's forehead, took the iron bar out of his hand. "Look here, Monsieur Surveyor, you're surely not going to ruin your own road!"

She kissed him furtively. We returned home, eating some pale grapes we had bought from a farm girl on the road to the village.

After their wedding, my parents moved to Provence. My father learned to love La Cadière. He discovered its mysteries, those far-flung houses about which people said, for miles around, that they pointed "the way to José's."

He made the distiller's acquaintance; they became almost friends. My father was wild about absinthe. I remember that he col-lected poems celebrating it. On certain evenings, he would read them to my mother in a low voice.

For several years he worked on the highways between Aix, Marseille, and Menton. He was gone for weeks at a time.

For his return, my mother and I would prepare the house. I raked the gravel path and put the dictionaries back where they belonged. I swept the dark staircase, whistling as I worked. My mother was beautiful.

My father always brought me a stone the size of his fist, and he would say: "Kilometer 34, from Aix to Marseille."

In my bedroom I kept a pile of all the roads in Provence.

When I was twelve, my father took me to Paris. We walked up the Boulevard Haussmann toward the heart of the city. I sat on the steps of the Opéra. We went into a famous café. I was intimidated. We sat down at a marble-topped table. A waiter came over, eye-brows raised, and said to me in a low voice: "Monsieur wishes . . ." Was that a question? I didn't know what to answer. I was served an orangeade with a few mint leaves floating in it.

My father pointed out a fussy old lady holding a spoon over her glass. "Look, she's drinking absinthe."

He added that in Paris the liquor inspired poets; there were poets in the salons, in the grand cafés, in the lowest dives. I didn't suppose for an instant that the charm of absinthe could be the same at José's and here in the capital. I was glad to return to Provence.

People living in the hills all knew José, whose cabin they visited to buy absinthe. More than the other distillers, he attracted such visitors. The climb to his cabin, the atmosphere of the laboratory, the tales he told, everything contributed to the spell.

The sun mingled its influence with that of the distiller. The absinthe gradually penetrated José's clientele.

Of this power of José's, nothing is left but a few vague lines in the report of 1911. When absinthe was prohibited, the Great War had begun a few months earlier. A long silence weighed on the hills. No one talked about wormwood anymore, nor about gentian; people forgot José. Only Médonin, before his departure for the asylum, still laughed about those gendarmes, Rouillet and Meunot, who had made their investigation five years before.

4

The notes I took after the war have disappeared. Certain episodes I had recorded have slipped my mind entirely. I have the vague recollection that around that time the distiller had hired an apprentice. Then everything bleaches out into sunlight.

One night, we had stayed at José's. My father had gone outside to get a breath of air. The distiller called to us. I was there alone with my mother. Her hair was pulled back, tied by a lavender ribbon. She was wearing a white dress.

José came over to her, as he always did. He looked at her, and said: "Good evening, Louise."

I think my mother smiled. She answered quite simply: "I enjoyed the story."

Then José added: "Louise . . . that's a pretty name." He seemed distracted. My mother took a step toward him. Her feet were bare in her sandals. José raised his hand. I held my breath.

The silence in the room increased. José caressed my mother's smooth hair. His slow gesture began at her forehead, continued down to the gentle swelling of her chin. José stepped back a moment. He smiled in his turn. Then he put his arm around my mother and, resting his hand just above her hip, kissed her on the cheek.

My mother remained perfectly still.

José went down into his laboratory. She stared after him. The little door closed. Slowly, Louise turned back and her eyes met mine. She seemed to give a start. I blushed, and so did she.

In such gestures, I saw nothing but the giant's kindness. The caress he had given my mother filled me with happiness. José liked the people he knew. His joy was a dialogue. My mother came over to me; she rested a silent forefinger on her lips and kissed me.

My father was waiting for us outside.

She had blushed, I remember that. This event describes José's distinct power over the people around him. I felt his force within myself.

Without absinthe, without Provence, would José have fascinated us so? I can't tell, I didn't know much about him.

Everyone wondered if he had really traveled. José never answered questions. He told stories. Or else he played a game with matches. He built tiny structures which swayed and collapsed.

When José vanished from the hills, my mother never said a word. In a letter to my father, which I also signed, in the summer of 1915, she simply wrote:

"Perhaps you haven't heard yet that absinthe has been banned. No one knows where José has gone. I thought he would leave word for us, or for the boy. But no, nothing. Isn't that strange? I'm still waiting for a sign; do you think he would leave without some message for us?"

During a walk, I asked my mother where the name José came from; I spoke jokingly: "José . . . That's not a real name is it? George? Joseph? Gérard?"

She smiled at me: "No, Jean."

I was surprised and, for no reason, I understood that José the absinthe-maker, the magician, the distiller, Jean perhaps, had disappeared.

5

Once, at the beginning of the war, I had ventured into the silence of José's laboratory. I was scarcely breathing; my eyes were not yet used to the dark. I heard nothing but the calm hissing of the still.

Groping my way, I approached the bundles of petals. Suddenly, one distinct word cut through the dark: "Absinthe."

I was startled; it was spoken quite delicately by a woman's voice I had never heard. I was shocked by the density of the word, and I stood perfectly still.

Like José, I almost never talked about wormwood. The two syllables I had just heard rose within me. In silence, I repeated to myself: "Absinthe, absinthe . . ."

I felt the first muffled syllable detach itself from the palate, extend in a delicate breath: the word's beauty was suddenly revealed to me.

Finally I glimpsed José, from behind. He was blocking my view of the person who had just spoken. I stepped to the side and saw a blond young woman, her lips held toward José. She repeated: "Absinthe."

It was as if it was the only word she knew. José set a lump of sugar steeped in wormwood between her teeth. His gestures were infinitely gentle. There was something uncouth about the young woman, who was half-undressed. Smiling, she repeated the name of the liquor once again. Her face was tilted toward José. The distiller held up a flask of absinthe: the green alcohol flowed over the young woman's hair, which he then pressed between his enormous hands. I stood silent in the presence so many mysteries. The shifting lights of the cellar concealed the unknown woman's face from me. But I think she was beautiful. I caressed her the way José had, in my mind.

I listened to the word endlessly repeated: *absinthe.* I was entranced. I closed my eyes; the liquor was born. It was that breath, that continual effervescence, that confusion of sounds. The absinthe flowed slowly over the young woman's hair and fell in tears at her feet.

I had the feeling that it was Marie. I recognized her transparency, her simplicity. Yet she had changed.

Gradually, I lapsed into sleep.

When I awakened, José was working at the still. I stood up, my joints stiff. He glanced at me, laughing: "What's the matter, *petiot,* too much sun?"

I couldn't imagine that the giant might lie to me. The light of the preceding moments was still in my mind. How could I have fallen asleep that way? What kind of spell... Was that really Marie? Could she have returned and finally gone down into the laboratory?

Returning from José's that evening, I turned around on the path; I thought of Marie, troubled by the dances of Aloé, and refusing to be present at the distilling.

Then I said nothing more. In the dark, the unknown young woman had taught me to listen to that penetrating word:

"Absinthe."

6

The memory of those years flows through me like a quiet tide. José has melted into the *garrigue,* between the pines and the brushwood. Marie has never come back.

The region itself has changed. Fire has stripped the hills. Sometimes there's nothing left but a few smoke-blackened beams. A child today would no longer have to search for the paths; he would merely follow the sloping line formed by the horizon of the mountains, ever higher.

La Cadière has remained a peaceful village. I say it without sadness: a strange form of desert has been created here. The population of the hills—hermits, shepherds, bandits—has come down into the valley. People have built bright little houses. Fine black roads have done away with the dust that rose under the cartwheels.

My parents' house, at the top of the village, was destroyed during the battle of Provence, in 1944. In the ruins, not long afterward, I discovered some old trunks filled with yellowed papers. There was José's whole story, from Argentina to Provence. It was my mother's handwriting, with additions and corrections by my father. I don't understand why both of them hid the truth from me, nor how those blue trunks could have escaped me so long.

That house was my last memory of childhood. With its disappearance, the story of absinthe is over.

7

Everyone knows absinthe. Some people still believe that you can drink it without consequences, and that it is an ordinary liquor.

Others compare it to Indian hemp, to the drugs from North and South America.

When I described José's life to my friends, several of them said, with a mysterious expression: "Oh, absinthe, yes, I've tasted that, it's terrible . . ."

Or else: "Not far from where I live, out in the country, one of our friends still makes it, in secret . . ."

In Provence, on summer nights, I walk through a sleeping La Cadière. The sky is quite black. I think of Jean Mardet.

Absinthe is one of those old words spoken too often to have any meaning.

Yet sometimes it manages to wake: fresh, light, new, full of enchantment for the soul.

THE
PROHIBITION

1

The spring of 1915 was bright. A pink mist bathed the hills. One morning, gendarmes were seen riding through the villages. They confiscated the absinthe they had discovered in the cellars, the cabins, the taverns. The distilleries were closed.

On March 17, the fabrication, the sale, either wholesale or retail, and the circulation of absinthe were forbidden throughout France.

By a strange irony, José remained the last distiller in Provence for some time. He was cited in the investigation of 1911, but was overlooked in 1915; his cabin figured on no record of the region.

Finally, a detachment of well-informed gendarmes turned up at his cabin, which was empty, apparently uninhabited. Yet I would have sworn that the night before it was in its usual state. The recipe books had vanished, as well as the secrets of distillation.

A search was organized in the hills. José must have been caught. No one ever saw him again.

2

Until 1916, Chief Sergeant Rouillet and Sergeant Meunot were assigned to maintain order in Provence, then in Bordeaux. Finally, they were sent to the front.

I don't know what their victories were, nor even their decorations. Their names appear on the French army lists, followed by the phrase: *Died on the field of honor.* At Choloy, dark enamel photographs have been attached to their white crosses. In that military cemetery where Rouillet and Meunot lie, glances follow you: a field of smiles, brave mustaches, proud glances, helmets, flower-decked kepis.

Meunot and Rouillet look almost alike: their faces are vigilant in front of the camera, as though surprised by the light.

The Fort of Joux will never regain the glory it knew in 1871. For a while it marked the border with Switzerland. Then the border was moved a few hundred yards into the forest, a winding path. The fort was demilitarized in 1965. From a distance, it preserves its grim severity, especially in winter. It can be visited in good weather, from nine to five. History students walk through the cold rooms making grand gestures. They tell how the young debauchee, Mirabeau, was imprisoned here by his father, and how he seduced the delicate Sophie de Ruffey, wife of the Marquis de Monnier.

They rarely mention the war of 1871, and no one has ever heard of Jean Mardet; no doubt they don't know that Pontarlier, where they are bored all winter, was once the capital of absinthe.

Buenos Ayres has become a great metropolis. It was a fashionable destination in the thirties. You met bankers on the run there, and a few bored diplomats.

The old alleys have been widened, a shining boulevard has been built along the ocean. Buenos Ayres has preseved its motley little houses and its remote charm. The city continues to attract travelers and to keep them by its delicious songs, its women in tango gowns.

Absinthe vanished during the First World War. Sufferings, then the joy of victory, have erased its very memory. Apparently vermouth is something like it, containing gentian . . .

In 1917 the Pernod Fils distilleries closed their gates at the east end of Pontarlier. An industrial warehouse was built on the site.

Then a chocolate factory, a long gray building, covered the fields. Today, you can smell whiffs of cacao deep in the woods.

Jean Mardet's first wife, Lise, died in 1924 in her mother's house. She lived alone for a long time. Her older son Michel studied medicine and practiced at Saint-Cirq-Lapopie. Thomas, after his marriage, managed a post office in Rouen.

I never found Anna and her child.

Absinthe.

It is easy, nowadays, to find in the Paris flea market one of those little pierced spoons that the wormwood used to drip through.

I'd like to ask one simple question, to which my researches in the official archives have discovered no answer. What became of the countless bottles seized by the French gendarmes after March 17, 1915?

Ten to fifteen thousand liters of wormwood were sequestered by the police from Pontarlier, Provence, the Aude, and taken in the direction of Marseille. But where were these cumbersome carafes of enchantment deposited, or destroyed?

3

After the war, Paris experienced *les folles années*. People forgot absinthe. The Grand Boulevards were magnificent for the Christmas of 1919. It was snowing that day. Everywhere people were dancing the fox-trot. Shapely legs were offered to all eyes, and the women's short skirts were an invitation to the party.